Belle

The Charming Gift

By Ellie O'Ryan
Illustrated by
Elisabetta Melaranci, Chun Liu
& Gabriella Matta

DISNEP PRESS

New York

Chapter One

*C*rash!

The noise thundered through the castle, followed by the sound of breaking glass.

"Oh, no!" Belle cried. She jumped up from her chair by the fireplace. "What happened?"

"I think it came from the library," Mrs. Potts the teapot said worriedly.

Belle rushed down the hallway. She hadn't

lived at the castle for very long, but she could always find her way to the library! It was her favorite room in the entire castle.

Mrs. Potts zoomed after Belle on a tea cart. Her son, Chip the teacup, squealed as the cart zipped around the corners on two wheels. By the time they arrived at the library, Belle was already inside—along with Lumiere the candelabrum and Cogsworth the mantel clock.

"Oh, my word!" gasped Mrs. Potts. "Whatever happened in here?"

"It must have been the storm," Belle said. She pointed to the window. A thick tree branch had crashed through it! Papers swirled around the library as icy wind and snowflakes blew through the broken window.

"Mama, it's cold in here!" Chip exclaimed.

"The castle records!" cried Cogsworth. "Hundreds of years of history!" He tried to leap into the air to grab some of the pages, but instead he fell flat on his face! Tiny gears and springs bounced across the floor.

"Hold on a minute, everybody," Belle said. "Let's not panic. First things first. We need to cover the window to block the wind!"

"There is a board in the closet," suggested Lumiere.

"That should do the trick," Belle replied. She grabbed the board from the closet and quickly covered the hole with it.

"There," Belle said, her teeth chattering. "Better already . . . even if it *is* a little chilly in here!"

"*Better?*" Cogsworth repeated. "Look at this terrible mess! It will take hours to put all these papers in order again!"

"Not if we all work together!" Belle exclaimed. "Lumiere, would you light the fire?"

"But of course," the candelabrum replied.

"A spot of tea will warm you right up, dear," Mrs. Potts said. She poured the steaming tea into Chip. "It will warm you *both* up!"

"Thank you, Mrs. Potts," Belle said after she took a sip of tea. "Hot tea is just the thing for a frosty winter day."

"Ah, ah, ah," Cogsworth corrected her, wagging his hand back and forth. "It's not winter *yet*. Not until December twenty-first."

"Of course." Belle laughed. "But it's hard

to remember that winter isn't here yet when it's so bitterly cold out!"

"Mark my words, there *will* be a lot more snow by morning," Mrs. Potts said wisely. "I can feel it in the air."

"That's all the more reason to make sure we tidy up the library today—so that tomorrow, we can play in the snow! That's one of my favorite things to do . . . after reading, of course," Belle replied. Then she turned to Cogsworth. "You must know all about the library's filing system. Where do we start?"

"Every item must be catalogued and cross-referenced. Then I like to color-code each item before I file them alphabetically by topic," Cogsworth reported.

"I have an idea," Belle said. "What if we start by organizing the papers by year?"

"I suppose that would work," Cogsworth said, nodding his head.

Belle gathered an armful of papers and carried them over to a warm spot near the fire. She soon discovered that the castle's history was almost as exciting as her favorite book! There was a tattered treasure map, and even a picture of a dragon that lived in the mountains long ago!

A few moments later, Belle found a golden piece of paper printed with fancy lettering.

"What's this?" Belle asked curiously.

Mrs. Potts hurried over and glanced at the paper in Belle's hand. "Ahh, the Winter Solstice Ball," she said. "Those were wonderful times—some of the best this castle's ever seen!"

"Go on, go on," Belle encouraged her. "I want to know all about it!"

"It was tradition that every year, on the winter solstice, a grand ball would be held to welcome winter," Mrs. Potts explained.

"Yes, the winter solstice," Cogsworth chimed in. "That's the first day of winter—*and* the shortest day of the year."

"The whole village was invited," Mrs. Potts continued. "Everyone looked forward to it all year long. As the sun started to set, the guests would begin to arrive."

"It might have been the darkest day of the year, but the castle glowed with light," Lumiere said. "There were torches lining the path—"

The honor of your presence
is most humbly requested by
His Royal Highness the Prince
at the
Annual Winter Solstice Ball
December 21
Sundown
The Grand Ballroom

"That made the snow sparkle!" added Mrs. Potts.

"And candles *everywhere* in the castle," Lumiere continued.

"The garlands were even better," Cogsworth said. "There were garlands of holly strung all around the ballroom."

9

"We laid the great banquet table with golden platters," Mrs. Potts continued. "There was every manner of food and drink that you could imagine!"

"What about dessert, Mama? Was there cake?" Chip asked eagerly.

"Of course!" Mrs. Potts replied. "We served chocolate cake and gingerbread and plum pudding and jam tarts! Oh, and cookies, of course. Hundreds of cookies!"

"Everything sounds delicious!" Belle exclaimed.

"It was," Mrs. Potts agreed. "But the best part was the dancing."

"Dancing?" Belle asked.

"Oh, yes, hours of dancing." Mrs. Potts chuckled.

"It was spectacular," Cogsworth said.

"After the sun set, all the guests joined the master on the balcony," Mrs. Potts explained. "The stars twinkled in the night sky as everyone gave thanks for great friendships. Then, the orchestra would play and the dancing would begin."

"How magical," Belle said, sighing. "I can't think of a nicer way to welcome winter. What will the decorations look like this year—or is it a surprise?"

"Well, you see, child—" began Mrs. Potts.

"Not since the transformation—" Lumiere continued.

"We could hardly invite the entire village here now, could we?" asked Cogsworth.

Belle understood what they were trying

to tell her. Long ago, a beautiful sorceress disguised as an old woman had begged to stay in the castle. When the prince sent her away, the sorceress placed a curse on the entire castle. The prince turned into a scary, ugly beast. Then the servants were transformed into household objects!

Ever since, they had been waiting for someone to break the curse: a girl who would fall in love with the Beast and teach him how to love in return. Until that happened, they stayed shut away in the castle, cut off from the village and the rest of the world.

Suddenly, Belle's eyes lit up. "I have a wonderful idea!" she exclaimed. "Let's have a solstice ball—for everyone *in* the castle!"

"But the solstice is only a couple of days

away!" Cogsworth cried. "We could never finish all the preparations in time."

"I think we could," Belle said. "Look at how quickly we tidied up the library—and all because we worked together. We can do it!"

"You're forgetting something," Cogsworth said. "What if the master doesn't want to have a solstice ball?"

"Shall we go ask him?" Belle asked.

Before anyone could reply, Belle was on her feet, clutching the invitation in her hand. All everyone could do was rush after Belle as she hurried off to find the Beast. No one knew what he would say!

Chapter Two

Belle rushed down the hallway. "Beast!" she called. "Beast, where are you?"

Belle looked everywhere—in the dining hall, the great room, the foyer, and even the kitchen. She finally spotted the Beast coming down the stairs from the West Wing, where everyone else was forbidden to go. The West Wing held one of the Beast's most precious possessions—an enchanted rose. As the years passed, the rose had begun to wilt, dropping one petal at a time. If no one fell in love with the Beast before the last petal fell, the curse on the castle would last forever.

"Oh, there you are!" Belle cried.

"What do you want?" the Beast snapped. Then he cleared his throat and tried to remember his manners. "I mean, what can I do for you?"

"I found this in the library," Belle said, holding out the invitation. "I was thinking about how delightful it would be to have a solstice ball this year!"

"Absolutely not," he said.

"Why not?" asked Belle. "Surely everyone in the castle would enjoy it!"

"Winter solstice—what's to enjoy about

that?" the Beast grumbled. "The shortest and darkest day of the year. That's hardly a reason to celebrate."

"I think it's *all* the more reason to celebrate!" Belle exclaimed. "Even the dreariest winter day is more cheerful when friends spend it together."

The Beast saw how excited Belle was and didn't want to disappoint her. "Very well," he replied, sighing. "But *only* for those of us inside the castle."

"Oh, thank you!" cried Belle.

"I hope you're right," he grumbled. His voice sounded grumpy, but everyone could see that his eyes had a slight twinkle as he looked at the big smile on Belle's face.

Everyone got right to work preparing the castle for the Winter Solstice Ball. Cogsworth supervised a parade of brooms, mops, and feather dusters, who cleaned the grand ballroom from floor to ceiling. Even Chip tried to help . . . but he kept slipping and sliding over the soapy suds! When they were finished, the ballroom sparkled.

Early in the morning on the day of the ball, Cogsworth tied a thick gold ribbon across the doors to the ballroom. Lumiere guarded the entrance.

"What's this?" the Beast asked curiously. He pointed at the ribbon.

"*Excusez-moi,* Master," Lumiere said apologetically, "but we must, ah, redirect traffic *around* the ballroom."

"But I always take a shortcut through the ballroom to get to the West Wing," the Beast argued.

"I am sorry, Master," Lumiere said. "We have finished decorating for the ball and would hate to spoil the surprise!"

The Beast was about to keep arguing, but then he smelled the scents of cinnamon, vanilla, and sugar. He followed the smell to the kitchen, where Mrs. Potts was almost finished making all the treats for the ball.

"Something smells delicious," the Beast said. He reached for a gingerbread cookie.

"Pardon me, Master," Mrs. Potts said. "They're not cool enough yet to eat!"

Then the Beast noticed a tall pyramid of cranberry tarts. "How about one of those?"

"They haven't cooled yet either, I'm afraid," Mrs. Potts told him.

"Mama wouldn't even let *me* have one," Chip added. The little teacup hopped over to a platter of red-and-white cakes swirled with peppermint icing. "But maybe we could split one of these!"

"Both of you, out of the kitchen!" Mrs.

Potts cried, shooing Chip and the Beast toward the door. "I was supposed to be at Belle's bedroom ten minutes ago!"

"Come on, Chip," whispered the Beast as they trudged out of the kitchen. "I have some chocolate in my study. A piece for you and a piece for me!" Chip grinned.

Mrs. Potts smiled. Normally, she wouldn't have let Chip eat chocolate this early in the day. But today—the day of the winter ball—was special.

"Stove, please keep an eye on the kitchen for me," Mrs. Potts called as she hurried toward the hall. "I'm off to watch Belle try on her gown. I can't wait to see her!"

Chapter Three

Mrs. Potts arrived at Belle's bedroom just in time to see her twirl around in her beautiful new ball gown.

"Do you like it?" Wardrobe, another one of the enchanted objects, asked eagerly.

"Like it? Oh, I *love* it!" Belle cried.

Belle spun around again. Her gown was made from sparkly gold fabric. Delicate long sleeves and a full glittering skirt added just the right amount of elegance.

"Wardrobe, you've outdone yourself," Mrs. Potts said.

"I just wanted our Belle to look wonderful tonight," Wardrobe said. "Now, for my favorite part . . . accessories! What would you like to wear, my dear? A necklace? A bracelet? Earrings? Or all three?" Suddenly, Wardrobe's drawers flew open to reveal trays of sparkling jewelry.

"Oh, it's all so lovely," Belle said as she peeked into the drawers. "How will I ever decide?" Belle slipped ruby and emerald rings on her fingers and looked through the jewels. Suddenly, she gasped.

"Is that a—?" Belle asked in excitement. But her smile disappeared as she pulled something shiny out of one of the drawers.

"Is something wrong?" Wardrobe asked.

"Oh, it's nothing," Belle said. "I thought this was a charm bracelet, but that was just a pendant lying on top of it. It's a beautiful bracelet, but I wish . . ."

"What do you wish, dear?" Mrs. Potts asked after Belle's voice trailed off.

"When I was a little girl, my father gave me a very special Christmas present," Belle explained. "He spent weeks working on it. Late at night, I could hear strange noises coming from his workshop, like the whistle of a teakettle and the clang of a hammer hitting metal. I had no idea what he was making!"

Mrs. Potts and Wardrobe both leaned in closer to Belle, captivated by her story.

"Then, on Christmas morning, I woke up with my heart pounding," Belle continued. "It was still dark when I jumped out of bed and rushed over to the Christmas tree. There, I found a tiny box wrapped in red paper. I was so surprised by how small it was. Usually, my father's inventions are enormous!"

Belle smiled at the memory. "My hands were shaking as I opened the box," she said. "Inside was the most beautiful thing I had ever seen!"

"Ooh, what was it?" Wardrobe squealed.

"A charm bracelet made out of shining silver," Belle said. "It had five tiny charms on it: a winter rose, a teacup, a sprig of holly, a star, and a snowflake."

"That sounds lovely," Mrs. Potts said.

"How did he pick those charms for the bracelet?"

"Each one had a special meaning," Belle remembered. "The teacup represented the warmth of friendship. The rose represented the beauty of love. The sprig of holly was a symbol of faithfulness since holly stays green all year. And the snowflake was a reminder that life is full of changes. The snowflake was my favorite."

"What about the star?" Wardrobe asked.

"Oh, the star? The star was for making wishes," Belle said. She turned to look out the window. "If I still had my bracelet, I'd make a wish on that star right now. But it's back at our cottage. I don't suppose I'll ever see it again . . . or my father."

Mrs. Potts and Wardrobe looked at each other. They could both tell how homesick Belle felt. They knew that she loved her father more than anything—that's why she had agreed to take his place as the Beast's prisoner. So it came as no surprise that she missed him more than anything, too.

"Well, it sounds like a lovely bracelet," Mrs. Potts said kindly. "I'm sure it would have been a beautiful accessory to wear with your new gown."

Belle nodded sadly.

Mrs. Potts frowned. She wanted to make Belle feel better. Suddenly, she had an idea!

"You know, I have some jewelry that would match your gown," Mrs. Potts said.

"You do?" asked Wardrobe. "I don't remember—"

"It's been in my family for years," Mrs. Potts said, interrupting Wardrobe. Then she turned back to Belle. "I'd be happy to lend it to you, if you'd like. I know how important family is to you."

"That's very kind," Belle replied. "Thank you."

"I'll bring it to your room before you get

ready tonight," Mrs. Potts promised. "And now, if you'll excuse me, I need to get back to the kitchen. There's still a great deal to do before the ball starts!"

"Come over here, dear," Wardrobe said to Belle. "Let's finish hemming your gown."

But instead of heading to the kitchen, Mrs. Potts hurried to the Beast's study, where she found the Beast and Chip sharing a bar of chocolate.

"I need you both to come to the kitchen," she said. "Bring Cogsworth and Lumiere. Hurry!"

"What's going on, Mama?" Chip asked.

"Is everything all right?" added the Beast.

But Mrs. Potts had already disappeared down the hall!

Chapter Four

$\mathcal{A}$ few minutes later, Mrs. Potts led the Beast, Cogsworth, Lumiere, and Chip into the pantry at the back of the kitchen. She closed the door behind them.

"What is going on?" asked Beast.

Mrs. Potts took a deep breath. "I've just come from Belle's room," she said. "The poor dear is feeling homesick, I'm afraid."

"But I thought the ball would make

her happy," the Beast said, frowning.

"Oh, I'm sure it will," Mrs. Potts replied. "But not even the ball can keep her from missing her home . . . and her father."

"What can we do?" asked Lumiere.

"Belle told me about a special charm bracelet her father made for her," Mrs. Potts explained. "What if *we* make Belle a new charm bracelet? She can wear it tonight. And perhaps it will help her to think of the castle as her new home . . . and us as her new family."

"But the ball is *today!*" Cogsworth cried. "How could we make it in time?"

"Belle's bracelet had five charms—a star, a snowflake, a winter rose, a sprig of holly, and a teacup," Mrs. Potts said. "If we each make one charm, then we might be able to finish it in time. And Belle ought to be busy enough today helping us clean and set up for the ball that we can make the charms without her finding out about them!"

"I could make the rose charm," the Beast volunteered.

"I'll make the snowflake!" Chip said excitedly. "I know Belle loves to take long walks in the snow."

"That's a great idea," Mrs. Potts replied. "I think I'd like to make the teacup, if that's all right with everyone else."

"I will make the star!" Lumiere announced.

"And *I*, the holly!" Cogsworth declared.

"What are we waiting for?" asked the Beast. "We'll find everything we need in the Royal Jewelry Chamber. Follow me!"

The chamber was located on the top floor of the West Wing. Mountains of rainbow-colored jewels sparkled in the golden sunlight: red rubies, yellow topazes, green emeralds, blue sapphires, purple amethysts, white diamonds, and black onyx. Long strands of gold chains and shiny pearls swooped along the walls. The jewelry was absolutely stunning!

"There's no shortage of jewels in here," Mrs. Potts said in awe. "Everyone gather what you need and try to finish by four o'clock. Then we can present the bracelet to Belle before the sun sets . . . and the ball begins!"

As everyone else searched the Royal Jewelry Chamber for supplies, Mrs. Potts

picked out a delicate gold chain for the bracelet. "This bracelet is *just* the right shade of gold," she said. "It will match Belle's dress perfectly!" Then she scooped up a small sack of jewels before hurrying back to the kitchen.

"Mama, wait! Wait for me!" Chip called as he scurried after her. "Can I help you?"

"Why, of course, my dear," Mrs. Potts said. "I've never made jewelry before. I'll need all the help I can get!"

When they arrived in the kitchen, they carefully placed all of the jewels on the counter. "Those are pretty, Mama," Chip said. "What kind are they?"

"The pale blue ones with the colorful specks are called opals," Mrs. Potts replied.

"They look like they have rainbows in them!" Chip exclaimed.

"That they do," Mrs. Potts agreed. "The purple ones are called amethysts. And the pink ones are rose quartz."

"Oh, Mrs. Potts?" a voice called from the doorway. It was Belle!

Instantly, Chip and Mrs. Potts scurried in front of the jewels so that Belle wouldn't see them.

"Y-yes, child?" Mrs. Potts asked nervously.

"I'm sorry to bother you, but I was hoping I could get a little snack," Belle said. "All the preparations for the ball are making me hungry!"

"Why, of course, my dear," Mrs. Potts replied in her usual friendly voice. But she gave Chip a worried look. He understood why. If Mrs. Potts moved away from the jewels, Belle would see them!

Chip took a deep breath and leaped into the air, turned a double somersault, and landed upside-down . . . right over the jewels!

Belle started to clap. "What amazing acrobatics, Chip!" she exclaimed. "I guess we're all excited about the ball, aren't we?"

"Here you go, my dear," Mrs. Potts said quickly as she offered Belle a scone with raspberry jam.

"Scones, my favorite. Thank you!" Belle replied as she left the kitchen.

As soon as she was gone, Chip and Mrs. Potts sighed with relief.

"That was close!" Chip squealed. "So, what should we do with these jewels, Mama?"

"I'm not sure yet," Mrs. Potts said. She tried to move the jewels into the shape of a teacup. But they looked more like a sparkling flower.

"Maybe you could glue them to something

that looks like a teacup," Chip suggested.

"That's brilliant!" she exclaimed. "I know just the thing, too. Wait here."

Pans banged and clanged as Mrs. Potts looked in one of the cupboards. "Here it is," she finally said. "This old cookie sheet is covered in burn marks. I can't use it to bake cookies anymore. So we can cut a teacup shape out of it instead! We just need one more helper to get the job done. Stove, would you do the honors?"

"Of course," Stove replied. He had a fiery temper, but was always happy to help as long as it didn't interfere with his cooking masterpieces!

Mrs. Potts and Chip balanced the cookie sheet on the counter. Then they held it in place while Stove used a pair of sharp kitchen scissors to cut out a teacup shape.

"Look, Mama!" Chip cried. "It looks just like a real teacup—only *really* tiny."

"Well done, Stove," Mrs. Potts said. "Now all we need is a little glue to attach the gems."

"There's glue in the study," Chip said eagerly. "I can get it!"

"You'd better take the tea cart," Mrs. Potts said. "We need to leave enough time for the glue to dry before the ball!"

Chapter Five

Chip zoomed off on the tea cart to the study, where he found the bottle of glue right away. But there was just one problem. Lumiere was already using the glue—and a lot of it! There was glue on the desk, glue on the floor, and even glue on Lumiere!

"Is everything okay?" Chip asked.

"I seem to be having some difficulty," Lumiere admitted.

"What happened?" Chip said.

Lumiere sighed. "I want my star charm to twinkle, just like a real star in the sky," he explained. "So, I cut a star out of paper and tried to glue these flakes of gold onto it. But the glue is too gooey and gloopy. The gold flakes are too clumpy and lumpy. And then my paper star tore in half. Now I have made a tremendous mess in the master's study, and I have nothing to show for it!"

"Maybe I can help," Chip said. "I was helping Mama make her charm. That's why I came to borrow some glue."

"That would be wonderful," Lumiere said gratefully.

"I'll be right back," Chip promised.

"I will clean up this mess while you're

gone," Lumiere said, flinging his arms out wide—and sending even more drops of glue flying through the air. "And then I will clean up myself!"

A few moments later, Chip raced into the kitchen. "Mama! Mama!" he yelled. "I brought the glue!"

"Very good, dear," Mrs. Potts said. "I've arranged the gems in a pattern. What do you think?"

A giant grin crossed Chip's face as he looked at the teacup charm. "Belle is going to love it!" Chip announced.

"Oh, I do hope so," Mrs. Potts replied. She carefully applied a drop of glue to the charm. Then Chip nudged a jewel into place and pressed it onto the glue. They worked together to glue every gem onto the tin teacup.

"That should do it," Mrs. Potts said finally. "Now we'll let the glue dry."

"Mama, can I go back to the study?" Chip asked. "I told Lumiere that I'd help him make his charm, too."

"Of course," Mrs. Potts said. "Remember, you still have to make your charm."

"I know! I'll have plenty of time!" He jumped onto the tea cart. *Whoosh!* It zoomed across the polished floor.

"No speeding in the castle!" Mrs. Potts called after Chip.

Chip knew he had to get back to the study right away. But what Chip didn't know was that Belle was on her way to the study, too!

"Whoa!" Belle cried as the tea cart nearly

ran into her. "Where are you going in such a hurry?"

"Sorry, Belle!" Chip exclaimed.

"That's okay," Belle said. "I just finished filling the ballroom with poinsettias. Since there were a few extra, I thought I'd put them in the study."

Chip gulped. If Belle went to the study, she would see Lumiere working on her charm . . . and the surprise would be ruined!

"That's where I'm going," Chip said quickly. "I'll take them for you."

"Oh, would you?" Belle asked. "Now I can get back to decorating the ballroom!"

When Chip rolled into the study with the tea cart full of poinsettias, there was no sign of the mess that had been there earlier. There was *also* no sign of Lumiere!

"Lumiere?" he called. "Where did you go?"

"Under here, monsieur!" Lumiere's voice called from beneath the desk. Chip peeked under it and found Lumiere mopping up the last drops of glue with a damp rag.

"Phew! I am finally finished," Lumiere sighed. "And I am exhausted!"

"I brought the glue back," Chip said helpfully, pointing at the tea cart. "Do you want to cut out another star and try again?"

Lumiere shook his head. "I have seen enough glue for one day! We will have to find another way to make the charm for Belle's bracelet."

"Okay," Chip said. "But how can we make the gold flakes stick to the charm without glue?"

"I don't know," admitted Lumiere. "We will have to think of a way."

"Think, think, think," Chip said to himself as he hopped around the study. He spotted a roll of stamps on the desk. "Stamps are sticky on the back!" he exclaimed.

"But *only* on the back," Lumiere pointed out. "I think the star charm should have gold on both sides. Don't you?"

Chip nodded. "Think, think, think," he said again. "Look! There is a bottle of ink in this drawer! Ink is sticky!"

"But ink is black," Lumiere said. "If the gold flakes get covered with black ink, the star will not sparkle and shine."

Chip knew that Lumiere was right, but he wasn't about to give up. Even so, as he searched the study, Chip had trouble finding something that they could use to make the charm. A feather pen, a stack of books, a pair of reading glasses, a lamp? None of these would work.

"Wait a minute," Chip suddenly said. He hopped over to the lamp and peeked at the waxy candle under its colorful glass shade. "I know what we can use!"

"What?" Lumiere asked excitedly.

"Wax!" Chip replied. He bounded over to the supply closet in the corner, where cakes of yellow beeswax were stacked on a shelf.

"You are a genius!" Lumiere cried. "Wax is *just* what we need to make this charm!" He pinched off a small piece of wax and gently heated it with his candles.

"Mmm," Chip said, breathing in deeply. "It smells like honey!"

When the wax was warm, Lumiere molded it into the shape of a star. Then he and Chip dusted the star with gold flakes. As the wax cooled, the gold stuck firmly to the charm.

Lumiere held the star charm up to the light. "Look how it gleams!" he said proudly. "This is just what I wanted to make for Belle. Thank you, Chip! You are an artist!"

Chip grinned at him. "I like to help," he said. "Do you think anyone else needs me?"

"You should check with Cogsworth," Lumiere replied. "I am sure that that overgrown pocket watch could use a hand!"

"Don't worry, Cogsworth," Chip yelled. He jumped onto the tea cart. "Here I come!"

Chapter Six

Chip zoomed up and down the halls of the castle, loudly calling for Cogsworth. Finally, he heard a familiar voice reply, "I'm in here! Come in, come in!"

Chip followed the voice to the greenhouse. Rows and rows of exotic plants filled the room.

"Hi, Cogsworth," Chip said. "Lumiere told me that you might need help making your charm for Belle's bracelet."

The clock hands on Cogsworth's face started to twitch. "That old wax-head!" he sniffed. "What does *he* know about it?"

Chip shrugged. "I don't know," he replied. "But I helped him make his charm, so I thought maybe I could help you, too."

"Oh, well, in that case," Cogsworth said quickly. "I suppose I *could* use a little help."

He stepped aside to show Chip a long line of leaves that he'd made out of jewels. "I came into the greenhouse for inspiration," Cogsworth explained. "And I've certainly been inspired . . . to make every plant *except* a sprig of holly! Look at all of these leaves! This one even has an acorn made out of rubies!"

"But you're supposed to make some *holly*,"

Chip reminded him. "Just like the charm on Belle's *other* bracelet."

"I know," Cogsworth said, sighing. "But there isn't any holly in here! And when I see other leaves, I forget what holly looks like— and make a different leaf instead!"

"There's a big holly bush outside, next to the fountain. I can get some holly for you," Chip said.

"Splendid idea!" Cogsworth cried.

Chip zoomed toward the large doors at the entrance to the castle. But on the way, he ran into his mother.

"Where are you going in such a rush?" asked Mrs. Potts.

"I'm going outside, Mama!" Chip said proudly. "Cogsworth needs a sprig of holly to make his charm."

Mrs. Potts shook her head. "The area around the fountain is covered in ice. It's much too slippery for you. No, my dear, you'll have to find another way to help Cogsworth."

"But, Mama—" Chip began.

"No buts, my dear," Mrs. Potts said firmly.

Chip frowned, but only for a minute. He knew two things: Cogsworth needed a sprig of holly, and he couldn't get it for him. He would have to find someone who could.

Just then, Chip heard a clatter. It came from the West Wing . . . the one place in the castle where he was forbidden to go.

And that gave him an idea!

Chip glanced around to make sure no one was looking as he hopped up the stairs to the West Wing. I won't *really* go inside, Chip thought. I'll just stand outside and ask the master to come out.

But when Chip arrived at the West Wing, the heavy oak door was closed. He knew that even if he yelled as loud as he could, the Beast probably wouldn't hear him.

So Chip took a deep breath and nudged the door open an inch at a time, until he could squeeze in. But he never had to call for the Beast—the door's squeaky hinges gave him away!

"Who goes there?" yelled the Beast. He leaped out from the shadows. "Who dares to disturb me in the West Wing? You know that you are forbidden to enter. Get out!" the Beast roared.

"I'm sorry," Chip whispered.

When the Beast realized that it was only Chip, his face softened. "My apologies," he said. "I shouldn't have yelled at you. I was just worried about the enchanted rose. It's already begun to wilt, so I don't want anything to happen that could make its petals fall even faster. What can I do for you, Chip?"

"Cogsworth needs a sprig of holly to make his charm, but Mama won't let me go outside because it's too icy," Chip said.

"I can get it," the Beast replied as they went downstairs. "A walk outside would do me good right now. It will be nice to take a break. And maybe I'll figure out how to finish the rose charm I've been working on."

"Do you need some help?" Chip asked.

"I might," the Beast admitted. "I just can't figure out how to make my charm look like a *winter* rose. Maybe the snow and ice outside will inspire me."

"I have an idea!" Chip exclaimed as the Beast opened the castle's front door. But neither one of them expected to see Belle on the other side of it!

"I was just hanging this wreath on the door. Where are you two going?" Belle said cheerfully.

"I need to get some holly for Cogsworth," the Beast said nervously. "But I think it might be too slippery outside for you, Chip."

"I can come with you—if you'd like company," Belle offered.

"Of course," the Beast replied, trying not to show how nervous he was. The Beast glanced back over his shoulder at Chip. "We'll be back soon."

"Bye!" Chip called as the heavy door closed behind them. He rushed toward the Royal Jewelry Chamber for a very important mission of his own!

Chapter Seven

When the Beast and Belle got back from their walk, it was time for Belle to start getting ready for the ball.

"Oh, my!" Mrs. Potts cried as the coat rack started to brush Belle's hair. "Look at all these snowflakes in your hair!"

"Your hair will dry soon enough," Wardrobe told Belle. "Have you thought about how you'd like to wear it tonight?"

"I was thinking that maybe we could pull the sides into a bun, and leave the rest of my hair down," Belle suggested. "What do you think?"

"How elegant!" Wardrobe cried.

Belle sat still as the coat rack started styling her hair. Mrs. Potts laid out Belle's shoes, while Wardrobe made sure that Belle's ball gown was pressed and ready. But a soft sigh made Mrs. Potts look up.

"Everything all right, dear?" she asked Belle.

Belle tried to smile. "Oh, yes," she replied. "I was just thinking about my father. I wish he could be here tonight. I think he would've had a wonderful time at the ball."

"I know he would've," Mrs. Potts replied. "And I know he would be very proud of you,

too. Why, there wouldn't even *be* a ball tonight if not for you! And that reminds me that I still have a few things to do. I'll be back soon in case you need anything."

"Thank you, Mrs. Potts," Belle said softly.

Mrs. Potts knew that she couldn't bring Belle's father to the ball. No one was allowed to leave the castle. But it *was* almost time to give Belle the charm bracelet—and she hoped that it would help her understand how special she was to everyone!

Meanwhile, the Beast had just entered the greenhouse, holding several sprigs of holly.

"Splendid, just splendid!" Cogsworth cried in excitement, spotting the holly.

"To add the berries, I need two rubies of equal size," he said, as he began arranging some emeralds in the shape of holly leaves. "Can you help me find just the right jewels, Chip?"

"Of course I can!" Chip replied. He scurried over to a large sack of jewels. But in his excitement, he knocked it over! A rainbow of jewels scattered throughout the greenhouse, bouncing across the floor.

"Oops," Chip said in a quiet voice.

"Oh, dear!" cried Cogsworth.

"I'll search for the jewels while you work on your charm, Cogsworth," the Beast said. "And Chip can pick out the rubies you need."

"Thank you, Master," Cogsworth said gratefully. The three went to work at once.

Chip was so busy finding the rubies for Cogsworth's charm he didn't even notice that the sun was starting to set.

When Cogsworth's charm was finished, the Beast and Chip stood back to admire it. "Well done, Cogsworth," the Beast said.

Cogsworth was so pleased that the clock

hands on his face spun around in circles. "Well, I certainly couldn't have done it without your help," he said modestly. "What about your charm, Master? How may I help you?"

The Beast nodded. "Take a look," he said. "I don't know how to make it look like a winter rose."

"I know!" Chip exclaimed. "That's why I went back to the Royal Jewelry Chamber. Look what I got for you, Master!"

The Beast and Cogsworth turned to Chip as he pushed a bag toward them. Chip nudged the bag until it tipped over. A small amount of shimmering powder spilled out of the bag.

"It's diamond dust," Chip explained.

"Maybe if you put it on the edges of the rose petals, it will look like frost."

"That just might work," the Beast commented. He held the charm very still as Cogsworth applied a thin coat of glue along the edges of each petal. Meanwhile, Chip made a neat pile of diamond dust on the counter. Then everyone held their breath as the Beast carefully dipped the edges of the rose into the diamond dust.

"Steady...steady..." whispered Cogsworth as they waited for the glue to set.

"What do you think? Is it dry? Should I turn it over?" the Beast asked nervously.

"Wait just another minute," Chip said. "Okay . . . *now!*"

In one fast motion, the Beast flipped over

the charm. The diamond dust sparkled and twinkled just like a fresh coat of frost!

"We did it! It looks just like a winter rose now!" cheered Chip.

"No, Chip, *you* did it!" the Beast said with a big grin.

"Oh, dear. What has Chip done now?" a new voice asked. Mrs. Potts was standing in the doorway, with Lumiere right behind her.

"Chip's great idea made my charm even better," the Beast said.

"That's wonderful news!" Mrs. Potts exclaimed. "You've finished just in time to give Belle the bracelet before she gets dressed!" Lumiere carefully cradled the bracelet, Mrs. Potts's shimmery teacup charm, and his own sparkling star charm. Cogsworth leaped forward to add his charm to the pile, too.

"Here is my holly sprig!" Cogsworth announced.

"And my winter rose," added the Beast.

"Oh, lovely," Mrs. Potts said as she admired each charm. Then she turned to Chip. "What about your charm, dear? Where's your snowflake?"

Chip's mouth dropped open. He'd been so busy helping everyone else that he had forgotten to make his own charm! The snowflake charm on Belle's old bracelet had been her favorite—and now her new bracelet wouldn't have one.

Chip had never felt worse in his entire life!

Chapter Eight

"I ruined Belle's bracelet!" Chip cried. Two big tears splashed onto the floor. "I promised to make her favorite charm . . . and I didn't do it!"

"Oh, dear me," Mrs. Potts replied. "There's no need for tears. After all, we wouldn't have my teacup charm without your help!"

"Or my star," Lumiere spoke up.

"Or my holly," added Cogsworth.

"Or my winter rose," the Beast said.

"It seems only right that *we* help *you* make your charm, Chip," Mrs. Potts said.

"Really?" Chip sniffed.

"But of course!" Lumiere responded.

"Come, come," Cogsworth urged. "There's not much time."

"The other charm was made from a sheet of silver," Chip said. "Can we hammer some silver for the new snowflake?"

"That might take too long," the Beast said. "We'll have to think of something else."

"What if we used wire instead of silver?" asked Mrs. Potts.

"There's a spool of jewelry wire in the Royal Jewelry Chamber," Cogsworth said. "I saw it this morning."

"We could twist thin strands of wire into the shape of a snowflake," Mrs. Potts continued.

"Perhaps we could add some beads," Lumiere suggested.

"That's a wonderful idea," Mrs. Potts said.

"Cogsworth, come with me to the jewelry room so you can show me where the wire is," said the Beast. He bounded out of the room. Cogsworth followed behind him.

When the Beast and Cogsworth returned with the supplies, they gave everyone a thin piece of jewelry wire. The group worked in silence as they strung silver and diamond beads onto their wires. When each strand glittered with beads, they twisted the wires together into the shape of a snowflake.

At last, Mrs. Potts held the charm up to the light so that everyone could see it. The delicate wire was so thin that it was almost invisible, and the beads glittered like crystals of ice. The charm was utterly enchanting!

"How beautiful!" Mrs. Potts exclaimed. "Chip, I think *you* should be the one to present the bracelet to Belle. After all, you helped make every single charm!"

Everyone smiled—except Chip—as the Beast dropped the charms and the bracelet into the little teacup. "Do you think Belle will like the snowflake?" Chip asked in a worried voice. "It's pretty, but it's not like the charm she had on her other bracelet. That one was made from a sheet of silver and it didn't have any beads and it—"

"Of course she will," Cogsworth said, smiling. "Now we've got to give Belle her bracelet before she finishes getting ready for the ball."

"Hurry, everyone," the Beast said as he glanced at the setting sun. "There isn't a moment to lose!"

As everyone left the greenhouse, Chip tried to smile. He hoped they were right!

Chapter Nine

Cogsworth cleared his throat, took a deep breath, and stepped up to the door of Belle's room. Then he knocked with three loud raps.

"Please pardon the interruption," he called. "Do you have a moment to spare?"

The door opened just enough for Belle to poke her head into the hallway. She looked surprised to see the Beast, Cogsworth, Mrs. Potts, Chip, and Lumiere standing there.

"Oh, hello, everyone," Belle said. She opened the door wider. "Please come in. I was just about to start getting dressed for the ball—"

"Ah, ah, ah!" cried Wardrobe as she whisked Belle's dress away and slammed her doors shut. "No peeking!"

There was a flurry of activity as the vanity table and shoe tree followed Wardrobe's example, rushing about to hide Belle's pretty shoes and accessories.

"Ahem!" Cogsworth suddenly said in a very proper voice. "Shall we get right to the presentation?"

"What presentation?" Belle asked.

"Go ahead, my dear," Mrs. Potts whispered to Chip as she gave him a little nudge.

The only sound in the room was the *plink,*

plink, plink of Chip hopping across the marble floor to Belle. He tilted his head down so that she could see inside the teacup.

"Why, what do we have here?" Belle asked curiously. Chip spilled the bracelet with all its charms into her open palm.

It took Belle a moment to realize what Chip had given her. Then she gasped in delight. "Is it—is it—?" Belle began. "Is it a charm bracelet . . . for me?"

"After we heard about the bracelet your father gave you, we all agreed you should have one to wear tonight," Mrs. Potts said. "So each of us made a different charm for it."

Belle clapped her hands. "Let me guess!" she said excitedly.

First, Belle attached the star to the bracelet. "The star gleams like golden candlelight. Lumiere? Did you make this charm for me?"

"It was my pleasure, mademoiselle," Lumiere said, bowing grandly.

"And this beautiful teacup, hmm, let me think. Mrs. Potts?"

"Right you are, my dear!" Mrs. Potts exclaimed.

Next, Belle picked up the holly charm. "Holly is so festive," she commented. "And I remember Cogsworth mentioning holly earlier. . . ."

Cogsworth smiled proudly.

"Just two charms left," Belle commented. "Oh, my goodness, look at this lovely rose all covered with sparkling frost! Did you make this rose for me?" she asked, looking toward the Beast.

"Yes, I did," he replied. He looked down modestly, but there was no mistaking the happiness in his voice.

"Thank you," Belle said quietly as she placed her hand on his arm. "It's beautiful."

Their eyes met for a moment before Belle, blushing, turned back to the bracelet. "And last but not least," she continued, "a snowflake charm! Oh, it's amazing! Look how it sparkles—just like a real snowflake. Chip, how did you ever make such a stunning charm?"

"I added a little extra diamond dust," Chip said. "Do you like it, Belle?" he asked hopefully.

Belle smiled. As she attached the charm to the center of the bracelet, her voice grew serious. "Chip, it's beautiful—the whole bracelet is," Belle said. "It's not the same as my old one, but that doesn't make it any less

special to me. Thank you. Thank you all."

Belle paused for a moment before she spoke again. "My father always said that the snowflake charm was a symbol for change," she said. "And my life has changed a lot since I came to the castle. I'm very grateful to have made such special new friends. I'm so very glad we'll be able to celebrate together at the ball."

Cogsworth suddenly ran over to the window. "The sun has almost set! Oh, the winter solstice is just about upon us—"

"Shoo, shoo!" Wardrobe cried. "Everybody out! Belle still has to get ready for the ball!"

Belle smiled as the Beast and the enchanted objects rushed out of her room. "Thank you again!" she called. "I love my bracelet so much . . . and I can't wait to wear it tonight!"

Chapter Ten

"Places everyone! Hurry now, there's not a moment to lose!" Cogsworth ordered. "Lumiere, light the candles!"

"Absolutely, sir," Lumiere replied with a salute.

"Mrs. Potts, make sure that all the food has been placed on the banquet tables," Cogsworth said.

"I'm on my way!" she replied.

"Master—hurry, hurry! You need to get ready, too!" Cogsworth cried. The Beast nodded and headed out of the room. "And Chip—you must go through all the halls and corridors of the castle. Tell everyone it's time to gather outside the ballroom. The Winter Solstice Ball is about to begin!" Chip jumped back on the tea cart and zoomed through the castle again. "It's time for the ball!" he yelled as loudly as he could. "It's time for the ball!"

As the sun finally dipped below the horizon, leaving behind ruby-colored clouds in the sky, everyone in the castle gathered outside the doors to the ballroom. Cogsworth paced back and forth in front of them, holding a large pair of scissors.

Wearing an enormous smile, Cogsworth cut the gold velvet ribbon holding the doors closed. Everyone in the castle gasped as the doors swung open to reveal the ballroom. It had been completely transformed! Crystal snowflakes and silver icicles hung from the ceiling. Statues that had been carved from real ice were scattered throughout the ballroom. Even the floor was so highly polished that it shone like a frozen lake.

"How lovely!" cried Babette the feather duster.

"Do you like it, *cherie?*" asked Lumiere as he swept her off her feet. "The decorations were all my idea."

"They were not!" Cogsworth argued. "Give credit where credit is due . . . to *me!*"

"Hush!" whispered Mrs. Potts as she stared at the doorway. Cogsworth and Lumiere turned to see what she was looking at and their eyes widened. Belle had arrived!

Everyone gasped as she entered the ballroom. Amidst all the silver and ice, Belle shone as beautifully as a sparkling golden sun.

Across the ballroom, the Beast opened the doors to the great balcony and stepped outside, motioning for everyone to join him. Hundreds of stars glittered in the night sky.

"Welcome, everyone, to the Winter Solstice Ball!" the Beast called out in his booming voice. He was wearing a fancy suit and looked very handsome. "Tonight we celebrate the warmth of our friendships and the light that they bring to our lives. So I bid you all: laugh, dance, and enjoy every moment of the ball!"

As several of the enchanted objects picked up instruments and started to play, the Beast strode over to Belle and gave her a low bow. "You look lovely. May I have this dance?" he asked.

Belle smiled warmly at him. "Of course," she replied.

They began to waltz through the ballroom as the others moved back to watch. Belle's charm bracelet caught the light whenever she moved, casting reflections of light throughout the room.

"Oh, don't they look *stunning!*" Wardrobe gushed.

"Wheeeee!" Chip cried as he zoomed by on the tea cart—straight to the dessert table!

"I'm so glad that the master agreed to host the ball again," Mrs. Potts said happily to Cogsworth. "It was just what we needed!"

"Indeed," Cogsworth agreed. "Care to dance, Mrs. Potts?"

"I don't see why not," Mrs. Potts replied with a smile.

The teapot and the mantel clock joined the feather duster and the candelabrum and all the other household objects, who were having one of the most enchanted evening of their lives.

And, of course, the Beast and Belle were there, too. Belle had arrived at the castle as a stranger, but she had quickly become a friend to everyone who lived there.

What a charming way to welcome winter . . . and to celebrate friendships old and new!

Don't miss the next Disney Princess Jewel Story!

Jasmine
The
Jewel
Orchard

One morning at the palace, Jasmine discovers there is no fruit at all to be found in Agrabah! She heads to the market to figure out what has happened. When a trail of beautiful amethysts leads her to the royal orchards, she learns that all the fruit and water have been turned into sparkling, shimmering jewels! It's a beautiful sight, but with no fruit to eat or water to drink, the people of Agrabah won't be able to survive. Will Jasmine, with the help of Aladdin and Abu, be able to reverse the spell that has been cast upon the orchards?